THE Berenstain BEAR SCOUTS

and the
Coughing Catfish

Look for more books in
The Berenstain Bear Scouts series:

*The Berenstain Bear Scouts
in Giant Bat Cave*

*The Berenstain Bear Scouts
and the Humongous Pumpkin*

*The Berenstain Bear Scouts
Meet Bigpaw*

*The Berenstain Bear Scouts
Save That Backscratcher*

*The Berenstain Bear Scouts
and the Terrible Talking Termite*

THE Berenstain BEAR SCOUTS
and the
Coughing Catfish

by Stan & Jan Berenstain
Illustrated by Michael Berenstain

A
LITTLE APPLE
PAPERBACK

SCHOLASTIC INC.
New York   Toronto   London   Auckland   Sydney

ISBN 0-590-60384-1

12 11 10 9 8 7 6 5 4 3 2 1   6 7 8 9/9 0 0/1

Printed in the U.S.A.   40

First Scholastic printing, June 1996

• Table of Contents •

1. The Mysterious Deep   1

2. King of the Cats   6

3. Lizzy's Complaint   12

4. A Gift from the Sea   15

5. "Help! Help! Come Quick!"   19

6. "Put a Cork in It, Fred"   22

7. Welcome to Saucer One   27

8. A Heavy Metal Problem   32

9. "How Do You Steer This Dang Thing?"   38

10. Up and Away!   43

11. Picking Up the Trail   49

12. Red Alert   56

13. Weak in the Knees   62

14. Gray-Green Ooze   67

15. Operation Bogg Bust   75

16. A Computer Glitch   79

17. The Hellion Queen   86

18. That's How Things Happen Sometimes   89

• Chapter 1 •

The Mysterious Deep

When the Bear Scouts stopped by to check out the pier at Lake Grizzly, they weren't surprised to find Gramps fishing there.

Scouts Brother, Sister, Fred, and Lizzy were checking out the lake because they were thinking about going for the Scuba-diving Merit Badge. They would need their parents' permission, of course. They would need Scout Leader Jane's permission. But most of all, they would need help from Professor Actual Factual. Help in the form of both instruction and equipment.

Actual Factual did underwater research. Not only was he an expert diver, he had lots of excellent equipment. He'd even invented some of his own.

Speaking of inventions, there was a rumor that the professor was gallivanting around the skies in a strange new flying machine — which might explain Farmer Ben's recent claim to have seen a flying saucer.

The scouts had just left their secret chicken coop clubhouse at the edge of Farmer Ben's farm, when they saw him jumping up and down pointing at the sky.

"A flying saucer! A flying saucer!" cried Ben. "I just saw a flying saucer!"

The scouts were polite as always, but they told Ben in no uncertain terms that they didn't believe in flying saucers.

"That's okay," said Ben, a little miffed. "I daresay flying saucers don't believe in you, either."

But it's one thing to think about the Scuba-diving Merit Badge. It's quite another to earn it. It was Sister and Lizzy who were all for the idea. Brother and Fred weren't so sure about it. They thought that Sister and Lizzy, who were two grades behind them, might be a little young for the challenges of scuba diving.

"What's young got to do with it?" protested Sister. "I'm at least as good a swimmer as you, and Lizzy can outswim you both."

"Being a good swimmer has very little to do with it," said Brother. "Scuba diving is a whole other thing."

"Brother's right," said Fred. "Scuba diving takes special equipment and training, and even then it can be dangerous."

"The trouble with you, Fred," said Sister, "is that you're chicken." She flapped her elbows like a chicken and said, "Puck, puck, puck-aww!"

"And the trouble with you," said Fred, "is that you've got more nerve than brains!"

"I resemble that remark," said Sister with a grin. Which she did, a little. Not that Sister was short of brains. She was, in fact, quite smart. She did, however, have an oversupply of nerve. It got her into trouble sometimes. Fortunately, the rest of the "one for all and all for one!"

troop was usually there to pull her out.

"What do you think, Lizzy?" said Sister. As was so often the case, Lizzy was off in a world of her own. "Huh?" said Lizzy. "What do I think about what?"

"About going for the Scuba-diving Merit Badge, of course," said Sister. "The thing we've been talking about for the last five minutes."

"Oh, I think it would be wonderful to explore the mysterious deep!" said Lizzy. "To swim with the fishes, to see the world through their eyes."

"Yeah, but what about sharks, sea snakes, and giant eels?" said Sister. "You'll look like dinner through their eyes!"

"Now who's chicken?" teased Brother.

"I don't think we'll have to worry about sharks and the like," said Fred. "Lake Grizzly is fresh water. Those species live in the sea."

"Lake Grizzly is connected to the sea,"

said Sister. "I know because I looked at the map."

"Doesn't matter," said Fred, who knew about such things. "The only time salt water comes into Lake Grizzly is if there's a drought. Even then, it only comes in a little."

"Look!" said Brother as the silvery sparkle of Lake Grizzly came into view through the trees. That's when they saw Gramps fishing from the pier.

• Chapter 2 •

King of the Cats

The reason the Bear Scouts weren't surprised to find Gramps fishing from the pier was that he fished there a lot. Gramps's goal was very different from that of the scouts. Gramps's goal was to catch Old Jake, the Catfish King of Lake Grizzly. Gramps was so gone on catching Old Jake that folk teased him about it. Even the scouts.

"Are you sure there's such a fish as Old Jake?" the scouts would say. "Are you sure Old Jake isn't just a myth?"

"A myth? A myth?" Gramps would sputter. "Old Jake's no myth! Old Jake's a mithter — er, mister. Mister Old Jake. King of the Cats. Brave as a lion, fierce as a tiger. Strong as a jaguar, with whiskers as sharp as a cheetah's teeth!"

"Have you ever *seen* this giant catfish?" the scouts would say.

"Seen him? Seen him? I've had my hook into him!" Gramps would protest. "Why, that monster has stolen enough of my bait to stock a grocery store. Everything from sweet corn to toasted cheese balls. I've been after him bear and cub for more than fifty years. Why, we've grown up together. You could say Old Jake and I have a love-hate relationship. I'd sure *love* to catch him, and I sure *hate* the fool he's made of me all these years!"

Then Gramps would see smiles creeping over the scouts' faces and realize he was being teased, and he would smile, too.

As the scouts walked out onto the rickety pier, they couldn't help noticing that up close the lake wasn't quite as beautiful as it appeared through the trees. It was still silvery and sparkly. The trouble was that some of the silvery sparkle was because of beer cans and pop bottles.

Lake Grizzly was the biggest lake in Bear Country. It was so big it had waves. Each wave left a little bit of trash behind: a foam cup, one of those trays French fries come in, some plastic straws.

"Just look at that mess!" said Sister. "It looks like the fastest thing about fast food is how fast folks spread their trash around!"

The Bear Scouts were fast food fans. They were regulars at The Burger Bear. But they were careful not to litter. It made them angry that other folk weren't.

But it's hard to stay angry when you're looking at something as amazing and beautiful as a great body of water. Lake Grizzly stretched out as far as the eye could reach. It was a thrilling thing to see. Surely great, powerful Lake Grizzly, with its zillions of gallons of water, could handle a few foam cups and a couple of plastic straws.

"I have a question," said Sister.

"So what else is new?" said Brother.

"What's this rickety old pier have to do with scuba-diving? Why are we checking it out?" she asked.

"Ooh, look!" cried Lizzy. "Look at the little fishies!"

Lizzy stopped and looked over the railing. Sure enough, the school of minnows, which had been flashing back and forth in the shallows, stopped and looked up at her. That's the way it was with Lizzy. Animals loved her. All kinds of animals. Lizzy could not only pet a skunk without

getting skunked, she once scratched a porcupine's belly without getting quilled.

"Come on, Lizzy," said Brother. "You can talk to the fishies on the way back. The reason that we're checking out the pier," he said, turning to Sister, "is that it could be a good takeoff spot if we decide to go for the Scuba-diving Merit Badge."

"That's an awful big drop to the water," said Fred.

"It is now," agreed Brother, "because it's low tide. When the tide comes in, the drop'll be just about five feet."

"I didn't know lakes have tides," said Sister.

"All bodies of water have tides," said Fred, who not only read the dictionary just for fun but knew a lot of the encyclopedia by heart. "Let me explain it to you."

"Please don't! Please don't!" said Sister, clapping her hands over her ears. She may have been teasing just a little. But there was no question about it: Fred, the great explainer, could get on your nerves.

Sister ran toward the end of the pier. "Any keepers, Gramps?" she cried.

"No keepers," answered Gramps.

• Chapter 3 •
Lizzy's Complaint

The scouts knew what that meant. As far as Gramps was concerned, there was only one keeper in Lake Grizzly. And that was Old Jake.

"Good to see you all," said Gramps. "Did you come out here to see me catch Old Jake? Because I'm gonna catch him, ya know." As Gramps spoke, he began reeling in his line.

"That sure would be fun, Gramps!" said Brother. "But that's not why we're here."

"Well, *I* don't think it would be fun," muttered Lizzy under her breath.

"What's that you say, little lady?" said Gramps. He had reeled in his line and was lifting it out of the water. "Bait's gone, dang it," he said.

"I said," said Lizzy, "I don't think it would be fun to see you catch Old Jake."

"Oh?" said Gramps, who was looking through his bait box. "Why not?"

"Because Old Jake never did you any harm," said Lizzy. "Why are you so set on catching him on that big hook and taking him away from his friends and family?"

"What do you mean, friends and family?" said Gramps. "Old Jake's a fish! And what do you mean, he never did me any harm? He's made a fool of me a hundred times over. He's stolen my bait, snagged my line. Friends and family, humph!" Gramps went back to shuffling through his bait box.

Sister took Lizzy aside. "Look, Liz," she

said. "I know how you feel. But Gramps has been fishing all his life. So has my dad. Yours, too. It's a guy thing."

"That doesn't make it right," said Lizzy. Sister shrugged. It was hard to change Lizzy's mind once she'd made it up.

"A bagel?" said Brother. "You've got to be kidding, Gramps."

"I've tried just about every other sort of bait," said Gramps, putting the bagel on his hook. "Okay, stand clear!"

Gramps drew his rod back. Then, with a mighty sweep of his arm, he cast his rig, bagel and all, far out into the lake.

• Chapter 4 •

A Gift from the Sea

The scouts watched as Gramps's rig —
hook, line, sinker, and bagel — splashed
into the sun-spangled water. The "mysterious deep," Lizzy had called it.

Lizzy was right. The deep *was* mysterious. Maybe that's why folk have been fishing for thousands of years. They fished for
food, of course. But it was more than that.
There's a kind of magic to fishing. A kind
of excitement. You never know what you
might catch: a little sunny too small to
keep, or an open-mouthed oyster cracker

whose teeth seemed to go all the way down to his tail — or even Old Jake, King of the Cats.

The scouts watched as Gramps jigged his line. "The idea is to move it a little now and then," he explained.

All eyes were on the spot where the line entered the water. What secret world lay beneath the bright surface? Were there schools of fish of every shape and size, or no fish at all? Was Old Jake lurking down there, or was he miles and miles away?

Everybody, even Lizzy, was staring at the line. Gramps tried to jig the line again. But it wouldn't jig.

"Got something!" said Gramps. "Got something big!" He gave the line a pull. "Something *really* big!" The line straightened as Gramps pulled as hard as he could.

"Maybe it's caught on a rock," said Brother.

"No. It's springy," said Gramps. "When I pull it, it pulls back. Rocks don't pull back. It's Old Jake, I tell you! It's just gotta be!"

The scouts rushed to the railing, except Lizzy, who held back.

"Easy, Gramps," said Fred. "You don't want to lose him."

Gramps was giving and reeling, giving and reeling, which is how you land a really big fish.

"I can't stand the excitement!" cried Sister.

"I can't stand to look!" said Lizzy, putting her hands over her eyes.

"I've got you now, Old Jake!" cried Gramps. Then, with a mighty roar, he pulled as hard as he could.

"I can't look!" cried Lizzy.

There was a shower of water and a big thump as Gramps's catch landed on the pier.

"Oh, dear! Oh, dear!" said Lizzy.

All was quiet as the others stared at Gramps's catch.

"You can look now, Lizzy," said Sister. "Gramps didn't catch Old Jake. He caught Old Bedspring."

It was true. When Lizzy uncovered her eyes, what she saw on Gramps's hook was a wet bagel and a rusty bedspring.

• Chapter 5 •

"Help! Help! Come Quick!"

"I'll catch Old Jake yet," said Gramps.
"You see if I don't. It was that bedspring
that fooled me. The way it fought when I
pulled."

"I hope you don't think I jinxed you,"
said Lizzy.

"Don't give it a thought, little lady. I
don't believe in jinxes," he said.

Lizzy breathed a sigh of relief. "Hey,
guys. I'm going to run ahead and touch
base with those minnows."

"Can I give you a lift home?" said

Gramps to the other scouts as Lizzy scampered ahead. "Got my pickup truck. But, say, you never did tell me what you're doing down by the lake."

"Thanks. We could use a lift," said Brother. "We're thinking of going for the Scuba-diving Merit Badge. So we're just down here checking things out."

That's when Brother was interrupted by someone screaming. "Help! Help! Come quick!" It was Lizzy. But she was nowhere in sight. She had been going toward shore, so there was no deepwater danger. Besides, Lizzy was a great swimmer.

The scouts rushed along the pier. When they got to where Lizzy had seen the minnows, they clambered down off the pier.

"Wait for me! Wait for me!" cried Gramps, who would have had a hard time keeping up even without the fishing gear. When he reached the spot and looked down, he was speechless. It wasn't because he was out of breath. It was because of what he saw. There, down in the shallows, with the foam cups and fry trays washing around their ankles, were the scouts. They were huddled around something so shocking that Gramps couldn't believe his eyes.

It was a fish. A huge catfish. A huge, coughing catfish.

It was Old Jake.

• Chapter 6 •

"Put a Cork in It, Fred"

"Don't touch him!" said Gramps, as he climbed down into the shallows with the scouts. "Those whiskers and fins are as sharp as razors!"

"I didn't know fish could cough," said Sister.

"He's not exactly coughing," said Fred. "It's more like a wheeze."

"Poor Old Jake," said Lizzy.

"He looks so sick," said Sister.

"I wonder what's wrong with him," said Brother.

"I'll betcha it's all this trash and garbage!" said Sister, kicking at some plastic wrap that had just washed up.

"Hey!" said Gramps. "This is no time to stand around gabbin'! Old Jake's in big trouble. We've got to do something! Run and get that tarp out of my pickup!"

The tarp was a big canvas cover that Gramps used to protect cargo when it rained. It was heavy. But the scouts managed to drag it down to where the giant catfish was flopping and wheezing in the shallows.

"All right. Give me a hand here," said Gramps. The scouts helped him unfold the tarp and smooth it out. "Okay," said Gramps. "Place yourselves around the tarp and take hold of the edge. You know, like the blanket toss at a football game."

The scouts did as they were told.

"All right now," said Gramps. "When the next wave comes in and lifts Jake, we'll slide the tarp under him. We're gonna have to be quick."

But the next wave wasn't big enough to lift Old Jake. The one after that was, and they managed to get him onto the tarp.

"Now comes the hard part," said Gramps. "We've got to lift him into my pickup."

"Hold it, Gramps," said Brother. "After we get him into the truck, what're we going to do?"

"Good question," said Gramps. "We'll think of something."

"I already have," said Brother. "The thing to do is take him to the Bearsonian. Professor Actual Factual will know what to do."

"Right," said Fred. "Besides being a chemist, a physicist, and every other kind of 'ist,' Actual Factual is an ichthyologist."

"An ichthy-what?" said Sister.

"*Ichthyologist,*" said Fred. "Pronounced

ik-thee-OL-o-gist: a fish scientist, one who is expert in the science of . . ."

"Later, Fred, later!" said Gramps. "Okay, everybody. Get ready to lift. One . . . two . . . three . . . LIFT!" It took all their strength, but they managed to heave Old Jake into the truck. "Now, sort of roll him up in that wet tarp."

"Won't that smother him?" said Sister.

"No, it's air that'll smother him," said Gramps.

"But that's cuckoo," said Sister.

"Not cuckoo at all," said Fred. "Let me explain."

"Put a cork in it, Fred," said Brother. "We've got things to do. You guys get up on the truck with Jake. I'll get into the front with Gramps. And keep wetting him down with that bucket of water."

Gramps put the truck into gear, and off they roared in the direction of the Bearsonian.

While all that was happening, nobody stopped to think how odd it was that Gramps was bent on catching Old Jake one minute and pulling out all stops to save him the next.

Nor did anybody notice the shadow that was following them as they sped along the road to the Bearsonian. It was being cast by a very strange flying machine that looked like a cross between an airplane, a blimp, and a flying saucer.

• Chapter 7 •

Welcome to Saucer One

The Bearsonian lay just ahead. It was
Bear Country's biggest and most important museum. It was a huge stone build-
ing with all kinds of towers and turrets.
Its great halls of science and nature had
everything from dinosaur skeletons to his-
toric inventions like Orville and Wilbear
Wright's first airplane. Its newest feature
was a special research aquarium. Actual
Factual had set it up to study certain
problems that were showing up in the
catch of Bear Country's fishing fleet.

"Drive around to the back, Gramps," said Brother. "We'll never get him up those front steps."

"How's Jake doing?" yelled Gramps.

"He's still breathing!" shouted Fred.

"Wetting him down seems to help!" said Lizzy. "But we're almost out of water!"

Gramps pulled to a stop and leaped out of the truck. "Fill the bucket from that hose bib, while Brother and I scare up the professor!"

"There's no way you're gonna scare up the professor because he ain't here." The speaker was Grizzly Gus, Actual Factual's bear of all work.

"Where is he?" said Gramps.

"Ain't supposed to say," said Gus.

"But this is an emergency," said Brother.

"Look here, Gus," said Gramps. "If you don't tell us where the professor is in exactly . . ."

Brother could see that Gramps was about to lose his temper. He tried another tack. "Gus, if you can't tell us where the professor is, perhaps you can tell us when he'll be back."

"Sure," said Gus. "He'll be back just as soon as he lands that new flying machine of his."

The shadow that had been following them appeared on the parking lot. Gramps and the Bear Scouts looked up. What they saw was like nothing they'd ever seen before.

"It's not a plane," said Brother.

"It's not a blimp," said Fred.

"It's not a flying saucer," said Lizzy.

"Yes. But what the heck *is* it?" said Sister.

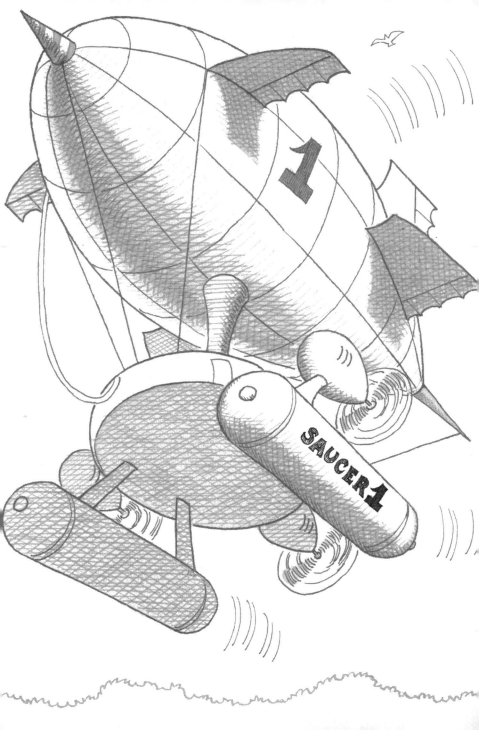

The strange craft that looked like a combination of all three settled onto the parking lot. The body was a thick, saucer-shaped, windowless disk with motors attached. Its landing gear consisted of two enormous floats. A rapidly deflating blimp-type balloon billowed over the whole thing. It wasn't exactly a big surprise when a door slid open and Professor Actual Factual stepped out.

"Gramps and the Bear Scouts!" said the professor. "Just the folks I've been looking for! What do you think of Saucer One, my latest and greatest invention?"

"Amazing!" said Brother.

"Remarkable!' said Fred.

"Fantastic!" said Sister.

"Totally awesome!" said Lizzy.

"Its full name is Saucer One in Service of Earth," said the professor.

"Hey, cool," said Brother. "But you said you were looking for us. How come?"

"You've spoken of your eagerness to earn the Scuba-diving Merit Badge. Well, I've cleared it with both your parents and Scout Leader Jane."

"Hey, *way* cool!" said Sister.

"Hey!" said Gramps. "Never mind 'Hey, cool' and 'Hey, way cool.' How about operating in service of a very sick fish we've got waiting in the truck?"

• Chapter 8 •

A Heavy Metal Problem

"Hmm," said Professor Actual Factual. "The lake is in much worse condition than I had supposed."

"Never mind the lake!" said Gramps. "What about Old Jake?"

"It's a clear case of chromium poisoning," said the professor.

"Chromium poisoning?" said Gramps.

"How can you tell?" said Brother.

"By the silvery look of the eyes, the color of the skin," said the professor. "And the wheezing, of course. I'm afraid I've been seeing a lot of it lately." The professor turned to Gus, who had fetched a wheeled stretcher from the museum. "Gus, take Old Jake down to the aquarium and put him in the isolation tank. And be careful! Those whiskers and fins can cut to the bone."

Using the tarp as they had before, Gramps and the scouts moved Old Jake from the pickup to the stretcher. He was still breathing, but that was about all.

"Professor," said Lizzy, as she watched Gus wheel the sick fish into the museum.

"Yes?" said Actual Factual.

"Is . . . is Old Jake going to die?" she asked.

"He's quite sick. But I'm sure we can pull him through. I wish, however," said the professor with a deep sigh, "that I could say the same for Lake Grizzly."

"Are you saying the lake is sick?" said Gramps. "The whole lake?"

"It's pollution, isn't it?" said Sister. "It's all that trash. It's a disgrace. All those foam cups and beer cans!"

"It's pollution, all right," said the professor. "But it's much more serious than trash."

"What's more serious than foam cups and beer cans?" Lizzy asked.

"Certain heavy metals," said the professor.

YOU MEAN LIKE ROCK MUSIC?

"You mean like rock music?" said Sister with a puzzled look. "I don't understand."

Nor did the professor. There was a little confusion until Brother explained that there was a kind of rock music called "heavy metal."

"Fancy that," said the professor. "A kind of music called 'heavy metal.' No, I mean real actual heavy metals: chromium, bismuth, lead. But in this case, it's chromium that's the culprit. Someone or something is poisoning Lake Grizzly with compounds of chromium. And it's up to us to put a stop to it."

"What if we don't?" said Brother.

"It will in time kill every living creature in Lake Grizzly," said the professor. "And after that it'll start on us. Because, remember, that's where most of Bear Country's drinking water comes from."

"Gee, professor," said Brother. "What are we going to do?"

"Let's put it this way. With the help of Saucer One, we're going to fly like a bird and swim like a fish — and maybe even do a little trash-picking on the bottom of Lake Grizzly."

Fly like a bird? Swim like a fish? Go trash-picking on the bottom of Lake Grizzly? It sounded crazy. But the scouts knew that Professor Actual Factual was crazy like a genius.

"But," continued the professor, "we're not going to do any of those things tonight. Tonight we're going to get our proper sleep. Besides, Saucer One needs to have its batteries recharged."

The scouts had gotten so wrapped up in the events of the day that they had lost track of time. The professor was right. It was getting late.

"So be here tomorrow morning bright and early," said the professor, "and we'll pick up the chromium trail."

"Do you want me along?" said Gramps.

"Absolutely!" said the professor. "You're going to be my copilot."

"You don't expect me to drive that thing?" said Gramps.

"You drive your pickup," said the professor.

Gramps looked at Saucer One. Its great disk shone pink in the setting sun. Its big balloon hung over the disk like a fallen omelet.

"That saucer contraption doesn't look much like my pickup," said Gramps.

"True enough," said the professor. "Well, good night, friends. Tomorrow is another day."

Gramps and the scouts climbed into the pickup and drove off into the twilight.

• Chapter 9 •

"How Do You Steer This Dang Thing?"

Gramps and the scouts showed up bright and early as promised. Actual Factual was eager to give them a rundown on Saucer One so they could take off on their pollution hunt.

"Not until I have a look at Old Jake," insisted Gramps. "After all, that's what this whole thing is about."

"He's nervous about Saucer One," said Brother in a low voice. "I think we'd better humor him a little."

"That'll be fine," said the professor. "The

batteries aren't fully recharged yet anyway."

The aquarium was a large basement room lined with tanks containing different kinds of fresh- and saltwater fish. Old Jake was in the big isolation tank in the corner. Gramps had to admit he looked a little better.

"At least he's not wheezing anymore. Well," said Gramps, "the professor is bound and determined to get us into that flying machine of his. I suppose we'd better get on with it."

Soon the Bear Scouts and Gramps were standing in the great circular room that was the cabin of Saucer One. The scouts were very impressed.

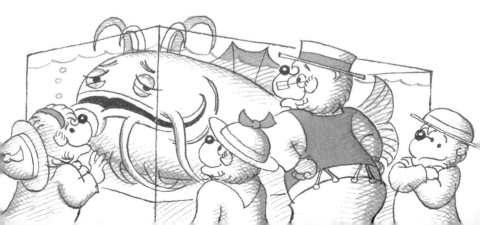

"Amazing!" said Brother.

"Way out!" said Sister.

"Totally awesome!" said Lizzy.

"I've never seen anything like it on TV or in the movies," said Fred, who was a *Bear Trek* fan.

"And these aren't special effects," said Actual Factual. "Saucer One is *real*."

Gramps wasn't impressed. "Real crazy if you ask me," he said. "It doesn't have a front or a back. I don't trust anything where you can't tell the front from the back."

The professor sat down in one of the twin pilot seats. "This is the front," he said. Along with the twin seats were twin computers with screens and keyboards.

"That may be the front," said Gramps. "But there's no steering wheel. How do you steer this dang thing?"

"With a mouse," said the professor.

"Are you saying this crazy contraption

has mice?" said Gramps. "Now I know I want out of here!"

The scouts couldn't help laughing. "Not that kind of mouse," said Brother. "The professor's talking about a *computer* mouse."

"Well," said Gramps. "I've made it my business to stay as far away from computers as possible. You know what they say about computers: garbage in, garbage out. As far as I'm concerned, this whole thing is a lot of garbage, and I'm getting out!" Gramps looked for the door, but it had closed so perfectly, he couldn't find it.

The scouts gathered around Gramps. "Please, Gramps," said Brother. "Don't you trust the professor?"

"Yeah," said Gramps. "I guess I trust him well enough."

"And don't you want to save Lake Grizzly?" said Fred.

"Yeah," said Gramps. "I guess I want to save Lake Grizzly."

"Look at it this way, Gramps," said Sister. "If we don't clean up Lake Grizzly, you'll never be able to go fishing again. But if we do clean it up and put back Old Jake . . . "

"I'll be able to go after him again, just like before!" said Gramps, his eyes lighting up. "Professor, shake hands with your new copilot."

"I don't get it," said Lizzy. "First Gramps goes all out to *save* Old Jake. Now he wants to clean up Lake Grizzly so he can *catch* Old Jake. I just don't get it."

Sister took Lizzy aside again. "I told you before, Liz. It's a guy thing."

• Chapter 10 •
Up and Away!

Just when it looked like the scouts had managed to settle Gramps down, there was another big upset. He was in his co-pilot seat getting steering instructions.

"It's very simple," said Actual Factual. "To steer left, you move the mouse left. To steer right, you move the mouse right."

Gramps was paying close attention. So were the scouts. The scouts had worked on computers. Especially Fred, who was a whiz.

The mouse was just a small gadget with a roller inside that you moved around on a rubber mat called a mouse pad.

"You see," said the professor. "When you move the mouse, the cursor moves. The cursor is that little red arrow on the screen."

"It looks simple enough," said Gramps. "But wait a minute. Where's the wind-shield?" He looked all around the cabin. "*Wait . . . a . . . minute!*" he said. "This thing doesn't have any windows! Not any! No windows is crazy! What do you do, fly blind? Sorry, professor, I'm outa here!"

Gramps unbuckled his safety belt. But before he could even stand, Actual Factual touched a few keys on his keyboard and a truly amazing thing happened. The whole solid windowless wall that ringed the cabin turned into a crystal-clear wrap-around window! Light flooded in. The

cabin was ablaze with morning sunlight.
Gramps and the scouts had to shield their
eyes.

"Too bright for you?" said the professor.
He touched a few more keys, and the light
dimmed a little. "Well, Gramps, is that
enough windshield for you?"

"I guess so," said Gramps. "We'll not
only be able to see where we're going, we'll
be able to see where we've been and every
other which way."

"How . . . how did you do that?" said
Brother.

"You know those sunglasses that get

darker in bright sunlight?" said the professor. "Well, I just improved on the idea a little. Okay, enough show-and-tell. It's time to take off. Take your seats, and buckle up."

Gramps settled into the copilot seat, and the scouts sat in the passenger seats behind the twin pilot seats. Actual Factual touched some more keys. There was a hissing sound.

"What's that?" said Gramps. "Sounds like some kind of a leak."

"No, it's just the helium generator filling up the gas bag," said the professor.

"Helium generator? That means you make your own helium," said Fred, who was a lighter-than-air buff. "How do you do that?"

"Reach around behind you, Fred," said the professor, "and get the salt out of the galley."

The galley was part of a bank of drawers and closets right behind the passenger seats. A very puzzled Fred reached back and found a shaker marked "S."

"Shake it into your hand," said the professor. "Okay, what's in your hand?"

"Salt, of course," said Fred.

"Yes, but what is it really? What's its scientific name?"

"Sodium chloride," said Fred.

"Correct," said the professor. "It's what you get when you combine sodium and chlorine, two very different substances. Sodium is a strange white metal that burns up in water. Chlorine is a nasty-smelling green gas. There's enough chlorine packed into that bit of salt you're holding to fill this cabin and kill us all."

The scouts looked at the pinch of salt as if it might go off like a firecracker.

"But put these two very different substances together and what do you get? Amazingly, you get sodium chloride, which is very good on sliced tomatoes and French fries."

The scouts were listening hard. But they couldn't for the life of them figure out what all this had to do with the hissing noise that was making them all nervous.

"Well," said the professor. "That's how we make our own helium. You see, I've discovered how to combine enough helium to lift Saucer One with another substance so that it fits in a space no bigger than your fist. The hissing is the sound of helium filling our gas bag. And when the bag is full . . ."

"We're going up! We're going up!" cried Gramps.

"Exactly," said the professor.

The scouts held on tight. Saucer One was up and away!

• Chapter 11 •
Picking Up the Trail

As Saucer One rose by the lifting power of
its self-made helium gas, Actual Factual
started the three motors that drove the
craft forward. The Bear Scouts watched as
the land slipped past beneath them.
Within minutes they were out of sight of
land. The waters of Lake Grizzly reached
out in every direction.

Copilot Gramps was having a grand
time rolling the mouse about on the
mouse pad. "Fantastic!" he cried. "This
beats regular driving all hollow!"

The professor was busy calling up maps on his computer screen.

"Looking for something, professor?" said Sister.

"Just trying to pick up that chromium trail where it left off yesterday," said the professor. "Yes, I do believe we're almost there. Watch the screen, please." He called up a map that showed the lake where the Grizzly River emptied into it. He touched some more keys and an "X" began flashing near the mouth of the river. "Steer for the mouth of the river, Gramps, while I touch base with the chief."

He put on a headset and turned on the speaker so the others could hear. "Saucer One to Chief Bruno. Saucer One to Chief Bruno. Come in, please."

The scouts knew the chief well. They recognized his voice when it came over the speaker.

"Bruno to Saucer One. Bruno to Saucer One. Talk to me, professor."

"Saucer One to Chief Bruno. We've picked up the chromium trail. We shall be descending soon. No sign of trouble."

"Bruno to Saucer One. Standing by as planned. Over and out."

"What was that about?" said Brother.

"Nothing really," said the professor. "The chief is a worrywart. He's afraid we'll run into the Bogg brothers if we go up-river."

"The Bogg brothers?" said Gramps. "We're not gonna tangle with them, I hope."

"What are the Bogg brothers?" said Sister.

"It's more than the Bogg brothers. It's the whole Bogg clan," said Gramps. "They're a bunch of gun-totin', bootleggin', barn-burnin' varmints who'd shoot you as soon as look at you."

Actual Factual touched some more
keys. One by one the motors sputtered to a
stop. "What Gramps is trying to say . . . "

"I *said* what I'm tryin' to say," said
Gramps. "Which is that if you're fixin' to
tangle with the Boggs, let's just turn this

thing around and head for home right now!"

"We can't do that, Gramps," said Actual Factual. "Besides, we're not fixin' — er, planning — to tangle with anyone. This is a very important scientific mission. The life and health of every creature in Lake Grizzly are at stake. We have to find where the chromium poison is coming from and put a stop to it. But, as I said, there's no reason for concern. The chief is a worrywart. There's no possible way the Boggs could have anything to do with it."

"If these Boggs are breaking the law," said Brother, "why doesn't Chief Bruno just go and arrest them?"

"Hold that thought, Brother," said Actual Factual. "I've got to reverse the helium generator. Let's see now. I touch these keys . . . and down we go."

"What happens to the blimp?" said Fred.

"It slowly deflates as it loses lift. Then,

when we're down, it folds into the saucer.
But I must control the process carefully
lest we drop like a stone."

Gramps and the scouts watched nervously as Actual Factual fingered the keyboard like a pianist playing a hard piece.

"There, that ought to do it," said the professor. "Don't want to make too big a splash."

"You ask why don't the police just go in and arrest them," continued the professor. "A number of reasons. Not only are they armed and dangerous, they're hard to get at. They live in a place called Skull Island, in the middle of Gator Swamp. It's a dangerous place. If the gators don't get you, the quicksand will. But more important: Nobody's got any real proof that they're doing all these illegal things. But there's no question about it: The Boggs are mean. They do, however, come by their meanness honestly."

"How so?" said Brother.

"The story is," said the professor, "that they're descended from Bagwell Boggs, the famous pirate, better known as Blackbear. He used to sail Lake Grizzly and winter upriver in the swamp. There's even a story that he lost his great treasure ship, *The Hellion Queen,* during a Lake Grizzly storm."

The Bear Scouts had been listening wide-eyed. They were all ears and imaginations as Actual Factual told about Blackbear and his sunken treasure. They were all seeing the same picture in their mind's eye: Blackbear's treasure ship rotting on a sand bank at the bottom of Lake Grizzly, skeletons wearing pirate hats, sabers encrusted with rust, half-buried skulls with fish swimming in and out of the eyeholes. Something else was coming into view in the murk. What was it? It looked like some sort of trunk. It had brass

corners. Could it be . . . *a treasure chest?*
The scouts would never know. Because
that's when Gramps broke the spell.

"YIPE!" he screamed. "WE'RE SINK-
ING!"

The startled scouts looked at Saucer
One's great circle of window-wall. They
saw green water rising, blocking out the
sky. Gramps was right. They *were* sinking.

"Please be calm, my friends," said the
professor as he touched a whole bunch of
keys. "We're not sinking. We're *submerg-
ing.*"

• Chapter 12 •
Red Alert

The Bear Scouts and Gramps shouldn't
have been surprised that Saucer One was
able to travel underwater like a subma-
rine. After all, Actual Factual had told
them they would fly like a bird and swim
like a fish.

Once they were over the shock, Gramps
and the scouts found the underwater
experience exciting and interesting. The
ride was so smooth that the scouts didn't
have to stay buckled up. It was a great
chance to study aquatic life. The scouts

were watching an amazing underwater ballet through Saucer One's window-wall. And what a ballet it was! Fish of every shape and size swam, flashed, and hovered in Saucer One's powerful underwater lights. There were lovely angelfish, grouchy-looking largemouth bass, schools of silvery snook, toothy pike, and needle-nosed gar. The scouts were in nature lovers' heaven. Especially Lizzy. She raced around the cabin "oohing" and "ahhing." It was all so exciting that for a moment the scouts forgot about the mission and poor sick Old Jake back in the Bearsonian's isolation tank.

But the professor hadn't. Not for a second. Saucer One's underwater sensors had picked up the chromium trail as soon as they hit the water. It showed on the computer screen as a big, flashing, beeping "Cr." Actual Factual explained that every chemical has its own symbol, and Cr was

the symbol for chromium. So there was no question about it. Saucer One was definitely on the poison trail.

But there were other questions. One of them was on Scout Fred's mind. He had enjoyed the underwater ballet very much. But what really turned Fred on was how things worked. What Fred couldn't figure out was what was powering them through the water.

Actual Factual was happy to explain. "It's really very simple," said the professor. He called up a blueprint of Saucer One on the computer screen and zoomed in on the landing gear. The flashing "Cr" was still there, but it was pushed into a corner.

"The floats," explained the professor, "are really miniature submarines. They take in water, then they compress it. Which means the water gets squeezed. That makes it heavier than the water around it. So we sink. The more we squeeze, the more we sink."

"I see, professor," said Fred. "But that doesn't explain what powers us through the water."

"That's even simpler," said Actual Factual. "We get our power the same way squids do. We just squirt some of that compressed water from jets. That pushes us through the water. As I said, it's really very simple . . . wait!"

While Actual Factual was explaining the pontoon system, he kept an eye on the "Cr" flashing in the corner of the screen. Two things had happened. It had stopped flashing and become a steady signal. It had also turned red.

"Gather round!" he cried. "We've got a red alert!" He touched another key, and the blueprint gave way to a big red "Cr."

"What's it mean?" said Brother.

"It means," said the professor, "that we've reached the end of the trail. The source of the chromium is just up ahead. It also means, I'm very much afraid," he added, "that Chief Bruno was right. It appears that the Bogg brothers *are* the source of the chromium. All right now. I'm going to send up the videoscope."

"Is that like a periscope?" said Brother.

"It's a periscope with a built-in video-cam," he said. "This is the first time I've used it in the field. So, I hope . . ."

"Won't the Bogg brothers see it?" said Sister.

"I don't think that'll be a problem," said Actual Factual. "It's disguised to look like a floating log."

All eyes were on the screen. A picture

flickered into view. It was a very long shot of what had to be Skull Island.

"Look!" said Brother. "There's a big rock shaped like a skull in the middle!"

"And buildings and sheds and docks all around! And Boggs!" said Sister.

"Lots of 'em!" said Lizzy.

"Can you zoom in on 'em so we can see what they're doin'?" said Gramps.

"It's already on full zoom," said the professor.

"So I guess we can add lake-poisonin' to gun-totin', bootleggin', and barn-burnin'," said Gramps.

"No doubt you're right," said the professor. "But I can't for the life of me figure out the how and the why of it."

"What are we going to do, Professor?" said Brother.

"We're going to get into our scuba gear," said the professor, "and *find out* the how and the why of it."

• Chapter 13 •

Weak in the Knees

When Actual Factual opened the closet to get out the scuba gear, a strange smell filled the cabin.

"What's that smell?" said Brother.

"Gator repellent," said Actual Factual. "Remember. This is gator country."

"Phew! It smells like my mom's perfume," said Fred.

"I guess that makes your mom safe from gators," said Gramps.

"Well, I think it smells nice," said Sister.

"And so do I," said Lizzy.

"Please, scouts," said the professor. "We've got business to attend to. Now, listen carefully. There's no time to go into the science of diving — buoyancy theory, pressure factors, nitrogen sickness. We can do all that later. For now, I'm just going to show you the equipment and demonstrate how to use it safely."

The professor demonstrated the gear by suiting up Brother in a complete outfit. It included wet suit, air tank, face mask, flippers, and life vest. The only thing Brother had trouble with was the vest. When he put it on, it almost knocked him down.

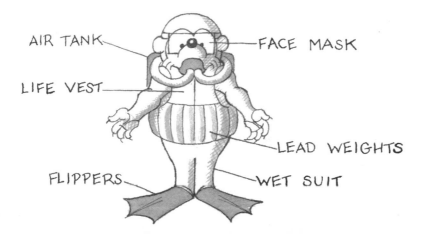

AIR TANK

FACE MASK

LIFE VEST

LEAD WEIGHTS

FLIPPERS

WET SUIT

"No problem," said the professor. "We'll just take some of the lead out."

"Lead?" asked Sister. "Why does it have lead in it? Won't that make him sink?"

"Too much will," said the professor. "But the right amount will make him weightless. When you weigh the same as the water you're taking the place of, you become weightless. Since cubs weigh less than water, we add lead."

"If you say so, professor," said Sister.

"It's true," said Fred. "That's where they teach astronauts about weightlessness. Underwater."

"I sure hope you don't expect me to get into one of those space suits," said Gramps.

"Goodness, no," said the professor. "You'll remain aboard. You will, in fact, be in command while we're gone. Before we exit, Gramps, we'll take Saucer One to the bottom. It's only about thirty feet deep at this point."

The scouts looked at each other. They *did* sort of look like powerful space creatures in their scuba gear. Powerful space creatures who were a little weak in the knees. They weren't weak in the knees because of too much lead. It was from *nervousness*.

Actual Factual looked *really* scary. He was loaded down with a big underwater flashlight and watertight radio pack, and he was wearing a special underwater wrist compass. He was going down a check list. "Let's see now, 'Gear check.' We've already done that. 'Lights.' Oh, yes, Gramps. Be sure to keep the lights on so we can find you when we return. 'Re-entry signal.' We need to signal you to let us back in. Let's keep it simple. I'll knock twice with my flashlight. Like this. Knock, knock."

"Who's there ?" said Sister.

"Orange," said Lizzy with a giggle.

"Orange who?" said Sister.

"Orange you sorry you came on this trip?" said Lizzy.

All Sister and Lizzy got for their knock-knock joke was groans from Brother and Fred.

"This is not the time for corny jokes," said Brother.

"Orange . . . you . . . sorry . . . you . . . came . . . on . . . this . . . trip?" repeated Actual Factual with a puzzled look. "Oh, I get it!" he said, laughing. "Not at all, Brother. A little humor relieves the tension."

Tension? A better word would be *terror.*

"You were talking about getting back in, professor. Well, I have a question. How are we going to get out?" said Sister.

"Through the air lock, of course," he said.

OH, I GET IT!

• Chapter 14 •
Gray-Green Ooze

The air lock was a big tank built onto the cabin that could be flooded and pumped out. It had two watertight doors: one to the cabin, and the other an escape hatch to the outside.

Once they were in the air lock with the cabin door closed, the professor turned a big wheel. Water began to flood in. When it was up to their waists, the professor had the scouts crouch down and practice breathing underwater using their scuba gear. It turned out to be so easy they couldn't believe it. Since they could neither speak nor hear in their diving gear, they couldn't do their "one for all and all for one" slogan. So they just did high-fives instead.

When the air lock was completely flooded, Actual Factual opened the escape hatch and led the scouts into the watery strangeness of inner space. They looked for all the world like a school of sea creatures as they flippered their way through the greenish water. There were no landmarks. Just water as far as the eye could see. Which wasn't far because very little light reached them.

The scouts stayed close to the professor, who kept checking his wrist compass and signaling them with his flashlight. They had gone a pretty good distance when a terrifying thing happened. Suddenly, a long black pole stabbed the water, just missing the professor. A dark shadow passed overhead. Then the pole pulled out and stabbed again a short distance away. The shadow was a flatbottom swamp boat, no doubt carrying a Bogg poling his way to some mischief.

It had been quite a scare. The scouts had lost headway and fallen behind the professor. He hovered until they caught up. He signaled them to follow him to the left. The water was getting shallower. They could see the bottom. Soon they were swimming through the stems of lily pads and water orchids. The bottom was coming up fast. When it became too shallow to swim, they swim-crawled. They finally reached the cover of the thick marsh grass that edged the river. There they knelt and rested.

At a signal from the professor, they slowly lifted their heads out of the water, pulled back their face masks, and looked around. Behind them was the river. All around them was Gator Swamp. It was all brown water, marsh grass, and dinky little islands for miles and miles. Some of the islands had shacks on them. Some had flatbottom boats, like the one that had frightened them so, tied to crude docks.

And straight ahead was a much bigger island. It rose out of the swamp like a giant fist. Atop the fist was Skull Rock.

The Bogg clan was hard at work in a cluster of buildings and sheds at the near end of the island. There was a system of strange-looking frames and vats. The center of activity seemed to be a huge, mysterious, layered pile of something. Every few seconds a burly Bogg would come to the pile, spear one of the things, and dump it into one of the vats.

What *were* those things? They looked almost like some great animal that had been squashed flat by a steamroller.

Other Boggs were working with scrapers and knives. Some of the things were being stretched on the frames. What looked like a giant faucet reached out over the river. Lumpy gray-green goo was oozing out of it into the water.

What *were* they doing? The professor, who was watching their every move, hadn't said a single word.

Suddenly, another boat was sliding by. Actual Factual and the scouts hunched down in the water. It was easy to believe that the fierce-looking Bogg poling the boat was descended from pirates. He had a dagger in his belt on one side, a pistol on the other, and a rifle slung over his shoulder. But it was the necklace of teeth that made him look truly fierce. *A necklace of teeth!*

Questions were racing through Actual Factual's mind. What was going on? What *were* the Boggs up to? Those teeth. What were they? Not shark teeth. Shark teeth are flat and white. These were curved and yellow.

Suddenly, it all fell into place. *"That's* what this is about!" said the professor.

"Easy, professor. They'll hear you," said Brother.

"It's an endangered species racket! They're killing alligators and tanning their hides to make leather!" said the professor. "Chromium is what you use for tanning! I should have realized it from the beginning! And those things on Skull Island are alligator skins, of course! Why, they'll get five years for every skin they're caught with."

"Don't look now, professor," cried Sister, "but one of those skins is coming near us! And it's got a gator inside!"

It was true. A huge gator was splashing toward them at great speed. It's amazing how fast an awkward-looking gator can move when it sees food.

"Don't worry," said the professor. "It'll stop."

Sure enough, it did. The huge gator stopped no more than thirty feet away. It sniffed the air, shook its head, and slunk away.

"My gator repellent," said Actual Factual.

"It works! Just like my mom's per-fume!" said Fred.

"Oh, no!" cried Sister. "The Bogg in the boat must have seen us! We're goners! He's pointing his rifle right at us!"

CRA-A-AK! The rifle shot echoed through the swamp. But the shooter *hadn't* seen them. It was the big gator that was a goner.

"It's time to put a stop to this!" said Actual Factual in a low but angry voice. He took the radio out of its waterproof case and twiddled some dials. "Actual Factual to Chief Bruno. Actual Factual to Chief Bruno. Do you read me?"

"Bruno to Actual Factual. Bruno to Actual Factual. We read you. Please come in."

"You were right, chief. It's the Bogg brothers, all right. It's an endangered species racket. Not only are they poisoning our water supply, they're killing every alligator in sight and tanning their hides. Over."

"Sit tight, professor. Operation Bogg Bust is on its way. Over and out."

• Chapter 15 •
Operation Bogg Bust

It seemed like a long wait, but it really wasn't. Within minutes Actual Factual and the scouts heard the chatter of helicopters in the distance. Within seconds six police helicopters were swooping down on Skull Island. There were choppers from as far away as Big Bear City.

The Boggs never had a chance. Police SWAT teams poured out of the choppers and rounded them up before they knew what was happening. Chief Bruno and his team had the outlaw clan disarmed and

handcuffed more quickly than it takes to
tell.

"How are they going to get them off the
island?" said Lizzy. "There are so many of
them!"

The sound of a deeper-voiced helicopter
was heard.

"Wowee!" cried Sister, as a huge trans-
port chopper came into view. "An airborne
paddy wagon!"

After the Boggs were herded into the big helicopter, the police began gathering evidence. The gator skins, the knives and scrapers, some chemical samples. They took pictures of the tanning vats and drying frames. Then they turned off the giant faucet that was oozing gray-green goo.

Chief Bruno was about to get into his helicopter. But he stopped and looked around.

"Maybe he's looking for us," said Brother.

"I do believe you may be right," said the professor.

They all stood up. They shouted and waved. The chief saw them. He waved back and made an A-OK circle with his thumb and forefinger, then he climbed into his chopper. There was a roar of rotors. Then, one by one, the choppers took off, with the airborne paddy wagon bringing up the rear.

"Don't you scouts have some sort of slogan you say to mark a job well done?" said the professor.

"We sure do!" said Brother with a grin.

The scouts looked for something to cross. There were broken-off cattails floating around them. So, there at the headwaters of Grizzly River, in the middle of Gator Swamp, in sight of Skull Island, the scouts crossed cattails and shouted, "One for all, and all for one!" Marsh birds wheeled across the sky. Beavers poked up their heads. Even gators took notice.

Then Actual Factual and the scouts pulled down their face masks, checked their breathing gear, and headed back to Saucer One.

• Chapter 16 •
A Computer Glitch

You wouldn't think a contraption as strange-looking as Saucer One sitting in thirty feet of water could ever look like home. But that's what it looked like to Actual Factual and the Bear Scouts when it came into view all lit up like an underwater Christmas tree.

They swam into the still flooded air lock, sealed the hatch, and pumped out. When the pressure in the air lock was equal to that in the cabin, the professor knocked twice with his flashlight. Gramps flung the cabin door open and gave the Bear Scouts a great big hug, wet suits and all.

Gramps had lots of questions, even though he'd seen the whole thing on the floating log videoscope.

"We'll answer all your questions, Gramps," said the professor. "But first, we have to turn Saucer One around and head for home."

"Are we going to swim or fly?" said Brother.

"We'll travel underwater, at least until we've reached Lake Grizzly. I want to take some more chromium readings on the way back. With the poison flow shut off, we should start getting better readings right away. And then we'll spread our wings — er, inflate our blimp — and fly away home!"

What a day it had been. What a *couple* of days! Little had the scouts suspected when they went to check out Lake Grizzly what excitement and danger were in store for them.

Something else they didn't suspect, as they relaxed in Saucer One's cabin, was that *the excitement and danger were not over.*

"Good," said the professor. "The chromium readings are falling already!"

The symbol for chromium was still showing on the screen, but it was no longer red and it was back in a flashing mode. Gramps had returned to the co-pilot's seat. Actual Factual had set the course, and they were headed for home. He filled Gramps in on the whole endangered species racket. He told him about the tanning vats and the drying frames and the chemicals. But Gramps still had questions.

"Where were you guys when the helicopters came?" said Gramps. "I was worried about you."

"We were hiding in the marsh grass," said Brother.

"We were worried about ourselves," said Sister. "We had some pretty close calls."

"Like what?" said Gramps.

"Gun-totin' Boggs, giant gators. You know, the usual stuff," teased Fred.

"Professor," said Lizzy. "We're going a lot faster than before. Why's that?"

"Before, we were going upriver, against the current," he said. "Now we're going downriver, with the current."

"You might say we're going with the flow," said Sister.

"Sort of like a tail wind when you're flying," said Fred.

"Exactly," said the professor.

The underwater fish ballet was still playing outside Saucer One, but the scouts weren't paying much attention to it. Not even Lizzy. They'd seen it before.

Still in their wet suits, the scouts were winding down after the amazing events of the day. But then something happened that would wind them right back up again.

"Drat!" said the professor.

"Something wrong?" said Fred.

"Nothing serious," said the professor. "Just some sort of glitch in the software."

"Hey," said Sister. "How come the flashing 'Cr' has turned into a flashing 'Au'?"

"That's the glitch," said Actual Factual. "It doesn't make any sense." He did a

major number on the keyboard. But the troublesome "Au" just kept flashing.

"What do you think it is, professor?" said Brother.

"As I said, it's merely a glitch," said Actual Factual, still working on the keyboard. "Perhaps a bad chip or something wrong with the mother board."

"If 'Cr' is the symbol for chromium," said Fred, "what does 'Au' stand for?"

"Fred," said the professor. "I think you know perfectly well that 'Au' is the symbol for gold."

"GOLD?" cried the rest of the troop.

"Maybe, just maybe," said Gramps, "we've happened onto the trail of that sunken treasure ship."

"May we look for it?" shouted the scouts, jumping up and down with excitement. "May we? May we? Please!"

The professor sighed. "I knew I'd regret

telling you that story," he said. "But I'd never hear the end of it if we don't at least check it out. But I must tell you I've located the problem. It's just as I suspected. It's a simple software glitch. You see, our sensors are set for heavy metals — substances at the high molecular weight end of the periodic table — and since chromium and gold are close in density . . . "

Of course, neither the scouts nor Gramps would have had the slightest idea what Actual Factual was talking about even if they'd been listening. But it hardly mattered because they'd stopped listening as soon as Saucer One picked up a great hulking form in its powerful underwater headlights.

"Don't look now, professor," said Sister, "but I think we've found Blackbear's sunken treasure ship."

• Chapter 17 •
The Hellion Queen

The Hellion Queen didn't look much like
what the scouts had pictured earlier in
their mind's eye. The great looming hulk
rested on its side between two underwater
dunes. There were no skeletons wearing
pirate hats, no rusty sabers, no half-
buried skulls with fish swimming in and
out of the eyeholes. And there was cer-
tainly no treasure chest. There was just a
huge sunken ship, its timbers sprung, its
ribs showing, looking like some great
wounded sea creature. Somehow it was

even spookier than what the scouts had seen in their mind's eye.

As the scouts swam in and around the wrecked ship, they thought about the ships of old, the mighty sea battles, the crew of this very ship sent to the bottom to become food for fish. It was food for thought.

They did find some "treasure": some plates, a few mugs, some knives and forks, even a crude spoon or two. They all were black with sea crust. The professor put them in a bag slung over his shoulder.

The first sign of trouble was a muffled grinding sound. Then it happened. Some invisible force — a powerful underwater current, perhaps, a shifting dune — brought the long-dead ship to life. With the creak of ten thousand rusty gates, the great ship, which had been lying on its side for centuries, righted itself. There was a swirling hurricane of sand.

Actual Factual and the scouts swam for

their lives. The last thing they saw before reaching the safety of Saucer One was the ship's carved figurehead. It was *The Hellion Queen* herself. Long buried in the sand, she had risen with the ship and was staring at them through blind wooden eyes.

"Well, did you find any treasure?" said Gramps, as he let Actual Factual and the shivering scouts back inside the cabin.

"Just these," said the professor, reaching into the bag and handing one of the plates to Gramps.

"Why, I've seen better stuff than this at garage sales and flea markets," he said.

But the plate was heavier than expected, and he dropped it. When it hit the floor, a bit of the thick black crust broke off. Beneath the crust, the plate was yellow — bright gleaming yellow.

"No wonder the plate was heavier than I expected," said Gramps.

• Chapter 18 •

That's How Things
Happen Sometimes

No wonder, indeed. Yes, the plates, the
mugs, the knives, forks, and spoons were
all solid gold.

There was great interest in what came
to be known as "Blackbear's treasure." It
was put up for sale at Big Bear City's
leading auction house. Bidders came from
all over Bear Country. The objects, which
turned out to be Blackbear's personal din-
nerware, were sold for more than a million
dollars. The buyer was Squire Grizzly,
Bear Country's richest citizen. The Bear

Scouts and the professor knew Squire Grizzly well. Not only did he live right there in Beartown, he was on the board of the Bearsonian.

The professor's plan was to use some of the money to raise *The Hellion Queen,* restore it, and make it the centerpiece of a small lakefront theme park. It would be called Pirates' Cove. All the money it

brought in would be used for the protection of Lake Grizzly.

The first thing the scouts had done when Saucer One landed was check up on Old Jake. He had done well in the isolation tank. When he was well, Gramps and the scouts loaded him into the pickup and returned him to his home in Lake Grizzly.

The scouts earned the Scuba-diving Merit Badge, of course. They decided to celebrate by paying their respects to Lake Grizzly. When they got there they saw Gramps way out at the end of the pier *without his fishing rod.*

"Hi, scouts," said Gramps when they joined him.

"How come no fishing rod?" said Lizzy.

"No need for it," said Gramps. "I said I'd catch Old Jake, and I did. No need to catch him twice."

The scouts just smiled. Lizzy went over

and gave Gramps a little hug.

"And there's no need to make a fuss, either," grumped Gramps.

A familiar shadow passed over the pier. It was cast by Saucer One. Actual Factual was still taking water samples. Gramps and the scouts looked up and waved. It's pretty hard for a flying saucer to waggle. But somehow Actual Factual managed to do it.

The situation at Lake Grizzly was much improved. The trash along the shore had been cleaned up. The new litter cans seemed to be doing their job.

The Bear Scouts looked out over beautiful, *healthy* Lake Grizzly. It seemed very strange how Blackbear, the pirate ancestor of the Boggs who had almost killed Lake Grizzly, was helping to save it.

But that's how things happen sometimes.

• About the Authors •

Stan and Jan Berenstain have been writing and illustrating books about bears for more than thirty years. Their very first book about the Bear Scout characters was published in 1967. Through the years the Bear Scouts have done their best to defend the weak, catch the crooked, joust against the unjust, and rally against rottenness of all kinds. In fact, the scouts have done such a great job of living up to the Bear Scout Oath, the authors say, that "they deserve a series of their own."

Stan and Jan Berenstain live in Bucks County, Pennsylvania. They have two sons, Michael and Leo, and four grandchildren. Michael is an artist, and Leo is a writer. Michael did the pictures in this book.

Don't Miss

THE Berenstain BEAR SCOUTS

and the Sci-Fi Pizza

Pizza twirling is a rhythm thing, and Papa really had the rhythm. First he twirled the pizza in his hands. Then, when it felt just right, up it went, spinning, twirling. Then he caught it, still twirling, getting bigger all the time. Then up again. Higher, higher. Bigger, bigger. Papa looked like a sure winner. He could almost taste that first prize: all the pizza he could eat, forever.

Then something happened that those who saw it would never forget. Papa's pizza went up all right. But instead of coming down, it kept on going up. It kept going higher and higher. It kept getting bigger and bigger, until it cast a shadow over the whole downtown.

At first the crowd watched in silent horror. Then they watched with screaming horror.

But it wasn't until the gigantic spinning, twirling pizza stopped going up and started to come down that the crowd got really scared. They ran every which way, screaming, "It's after us! It's after us!"

"I've got news for them," said Brother to Gramps and his fellow scouts. "It's not after them. It's after us. SO RUN FOR YOUR LIVES!"

You're about to meet the biggest bug this side of Bear Country!

THE Berenstain® BEAR SCOUTS and the TERRIBLE TALKING TERMITE

by Stan & Jan Berenstain

Isn't it funny that as soon as picnic tables, chairs, and fences start disappearing in Bear Country, Super Swindler Ralph Ripoff starts selling termite insurance? The Bear Scouts think so. Can they turn the tables on Ralph before the terrible termite tears up the town?

Coming in June

BBRTT1195

THE Berenstain BEAR® SCOUTS
by Stan & Jan Berenstain

Don't miss the Berenstain Bear Scouts' other exciting adventures!

Join Scouts Brother, Sister, Fred, and Lizzy as they defend the weak, catch the crooked, joust against the unjust, and rally against rottenness of all kinds!

☐ BBF60383-3	The Berenstain Bear Scouts and the Coughing Catfish	$2.99
☐ BBF60380-9	The Berenstain Bear Scouts and the Humongous Pumpkin	$2.99
☐ BBF60384-1	The Berenstain Bear Scouts and the Terrible Talking Termite	$2.99
☐ BBF60379-5	The Berenstain Bear Scouts in Giant Bat Cave	$2.99
☐ BBF60381-7	The Berenstain Bear Scouts Meet Bigpaw	$2.99
☐ BBF60382-5	The Berenstain Bear Scouts Save That Backscratcher	$2.99

© 1995 Berenstain Enterprises, Inc.

Available wherever you buy books or use this order form.

- -

Send orders to:
Scholastic Inc., P.O. Box 7502, 2931 East McCarty Street, Jefferson City, MO 65102-7502

Please send me the books I have checked above. I am enclosing $_____ (please add $2.00 to cover shipping and handling). Send check or money order — no cash or C.O.D.s please.

Name___James Pelz_____ Birthdate___/___/___
                                       M   D   Y

Address___4273_____

City___Carson City___ State_Navada_Zip_____

Please allow four to six weeks for delivery. Offer good in U.S.A. only. Sorry, mail orders are not available to residents of Canada. Prices subject to change.

BBR1195